BUTTON EYES, NO EYES

Button Eyes, No Eyes
Copyright © 2024 by Mone't Tyson

Published in the United States of America

Library of Congress Control Number: 2024911809
ISBN   Paperback: 979-8-89091-790-4
ISBN   eBook: 979-8-89091-791-1

All rights reserved. No part of this publication may be reproduced, stored in a retrieval system or transmitted in any way by any means, electronic, mechanical, photocopy, recording or otherwise without the prior permission of the author except as provided by USA copyright law.

The opinions expressed by the author are not necessarily those of ReadersMagnet, LLC.

ReadersMagnet, LLC
10620 Treena Street, Suite 230
San Diego, California, 92131 USA
1.619. 354. 2643 | www.readersmagnet.com

Book design copyright © 2024 by ReadersMagnet, LLC. All rights reserved.

Cover design by Tifanny Curaza
Interior design by Don De Guzman

BUTTON EYES, NO EYES

MONE'T TYSON

Where to find the author:

Wattpad: @Monettyson.
Pinterest: @ShiningDreamingly.
YouTube: @ShiningDreamingly.
Zepeto: @ShiningDreamingly.
TikTok: @ShiningDreamingly.

BUTTON EYES, NO EYES

"Everything is a mystery in my life, but the question is can I solve it before it's too late?"

CHAPTER 1

Have you ever heard the story, about the Button Eyes and the No Eyes? Well, they don't really tell our story but just theirs. Since you may not have heard, maybe it should be told to you readers, out there.

You see, when I was younger, my mother used to talk about those who didn't have any eyes. It was my favorite bedtime story she ever told me.

She would tell me everything about them— about how some are good and bad, how even with no eyes, they could still see us.

No one knows how they can see us, or even see things, but anything is possible in the world I live in right? I found

it weird because no one, including me, was able to find them. No matter how many times you search for them, they cannot be found! But why?

If I'm being honest, the story I so dearly loved -- one night, I heard no more of it.

Because of him.

CHAPTER 2

My father.

He was the one who made my mother stop telling me the stories about them. He always hated the No Eyes, even when he never met one himself.

*"I heard enough; she doesn't need to hear anymore," he would always say. My father was very cold and sometimes I wondered how this man could be my **father**. The one who stood against the door was Grayson, I was told that he gave birth to me.*

My mother stood up, rolling her eyes. Why? That's easy, because my father rushed her to leave my room. Knowing them, they were possibly going to argue once again.

Before she walked out the door, she smiled at me softly. Even at my age, Mother was never happy.

"Mama, can't you finish telling the story tonight? You never tell me everything," I said selfishly.

"Maybe another time, honey, now please go to sleep," she said, kissing my forehead goodnight.

"Goodnight."

The moment the lights were off in my room and the door closed, I was sleeping like Sleeping Beauty.

Little did I know that the bedtime story I loved to hear caused argument after argument. Everything would become so much worse than it already was.

CHAPTER 3

What was worse, he made me never want to hear about No Eyes again.

*Afterwards, my father took my mother out for dinner which I thought was nice. The weird part was that he came back **without her**.*

Mother was no longer around or with him, but how could that be?

"Where's Mama?" I asked worriedly.

"Gone," he coldly said, trying not to speak about what may have happened. I'm sorry to say, but who would trust this man or figure out what he was up to?

Me, duh. Who else?

"What do you mean Mama's gone?" I asked. Those words he spoke next were the biggest and most shocking thing I've ever heard.

I wish I hadn't heard them, praying it wasn't true.

"She's dead."

CHAPTER 4

"No, she can't be-"

My voice became very shaky, dry, and my eyes became watery.

He had to be lying to me, right? Or playing some sick joke? There was no way this man could be telling the truth.

I mean, where was the proof that she was de-dead... When I started crying, he became angry at me.

You may all be wondering why?

He was upset because I treated my mother like she was the only person in my life who truly understood me.

"STOP ACTING LIKE I'M NOT YOUR FATHER AND STOP LOOKING FOR THAT STUPID MOTHER OF YOURS. I AM PART OF THIS FAMILY, TOO. DO YOU

UNDERSTAND BRAT?!" he yelled, roughly grabbing my arm, dragging me into my room.

I kept yelling back, telling him to let go because he was making me cry and hurting me. In that very moment, I hoped that a miracle would happen and all of this would end.

I was hoping someone would save me from this monster of a man.

He was blaming me for trying to find out why my mother had died. I'm pretty sure anyone would react the same way or worse. There were no last words of goodbye, she

was just gone, Forever.

One thing though... **who killed her?**

That was the question that must be answered. Who knows, maybe it was him, **Grayson.**

It would all make sense since he was with her last. Plus, he seemed to hate my mother so much, but wasn't he in love with her?

What changed in him to stop?

"NOW, SHUT UP BRAT!" He threw me into my room, putting a chair in front of my door, so I wouldn't be able to get out.

Now for the rest of my life, I have to deal with this father of mine, but everything can change the moment I turn 17

CHAPTER 5

Hello, my name is Chrysan. It's a beautiful and pretty name. The name means beautiful, lively, spirited, and a goddess.

Kidding. It's just a joke. The meaning is only beautiful, don't worry.

*I'm older now and guess what? Today is February 14*th *and we know what that means.*

MY BIRTHDAY.

Oh, and its Valentine's day, too.

"Happy birthday, Chrysan!" my two best friends, Nova and Blossom cheerfully said, hugging me all at once.

We all sat down on some rocks next to us, talking.

"How does it feel to finally be 17 knowing you're the youngest one out of us?" Nova asked.

"It feels amazing being 17 now, but I don't want to feel too old like you guys."

We laughed.

"If you ever met the No Eyes people one day, I bet they would truly love you, because what's not to love about

you?" Blossom said, causing me to question if they would truly love me.

"Wait— have you heard the story about them, Chrysan?" Nova asked, and I nodded my head.

"How do you find them? Does anyone know or—"

They both shook their heads and I was left with disappointment on my face. If only my mother were still

alive maybe she would have known where or how to find them.

"I did hear something about them, but I'm not sure if it's true.

It was said, that if you end up being the chosen one, you'll wake up in their world once you fall asleep."

"The chosen one for what?" I asked curiously.

They obviously didn't know.

Within seconds, we stopped talking and had a small birthday party for me in the forest.

It was fun, but time flies by when you're having fun. Nova and Blossom decided to clean up.

I hurried home before my father could arrive. I couldn't let him get home before me, or who knows what might happen to me.

He had people watching me and some weren't that friendly. The moment I arrived home, I went straight to take a shower, so I could get in my comfortable bed.

Of course, I locked my door, so he wouldn't wake me up from my sleep.

As I lay down in my bed and slowly closed my eyes—

I woke up.

CHAPTER 6

I woke up somewhere— I didn't recognize the place, but wherever I was, it was surely beautiful.

"Isn't it nighttime right now?" I quietly said to myself, getting up from the ground where I was supposed to be sleeping and I walked to find people.

Maybe someone could tell me where I was or how to get back home. I kept walking and walking, but stopped as soon as I saw them.

"The ones with no eyes."

A shocked expression appeared on my face and my words attracted their attention.

For some reason they were afraid of me and dropped everything.

Most of them ran away, but some stood there in shock. Guards suddenly appeared, pointing weapons at me like I was an enemy or threat.

My hands went up as they came closer to me with their weapons.

"HOW DID YOU GET HERE?! LEAVE NOW! YOU AREN'T WELCOME HERE!"

"I don't want to harm any of you. I'm not sure how I got here. I only came to ask for help, so I can go back home." I said, kneeling on both knees.

"Is that true, dear?"

A beautiful voice spoke. It sounded like a woman and as I slowly looked up, she wasn't just any woman, but she appeared to be the queen of this place.

CHAPTER 7

Everything about her showed that she was the queen. I nodded.

She grabbed my hand gently and helped me to get up on my feet.

"Follow me dear and everyone else please do not fear, we are not in any danger." Everyone calmly went back to what they were doing.

We arrived at the castle a little later and it was the most beautiful castle I had ever seen.

The queen herself took me into a meeting room where we both sat down and shortly after people entered the room.

These people seemed very important and my existence here made it worse.

They didn't know who I was, or why I was here.

Everything felt intense, which made me scared for my life.

"Are you guys going to hurt me?" I bluntly said, tired of the silence. Instead of them being rude or mean to me, they all laughed.

*My attention went towards the door when a **handsome guy** walked in and didn't laugh at all.*

"You sound like an idiot. If we wanted to kill or hurt you, we would have done it already." The guy was really cold, but for some weird reason he was attractive.

"Don't be mean to our guests." "Whatever."

The queen looked at me and said "Dear, I am Queen Widow and this is my husband Shadow, who is the king of this kingdom and beside him is my son, Sirius."

"My name is Chrysan and as you can see, I'm a Button Eye. Nice to meet everyone."

"Very pretty name, dear. What do you think, Sirius?"

"Why would I care about this idiot's name?"

"You don't have to be so mean. You know nothing about me." I spoke rudely to him. He smirked and walked towards me.

His dark eyes with nothing in them looked at me up and down. When he lifted my chin, leaning close to my lips like he was about to kiss me.

At the last minute, he backed away from me. Why? Did he have to tease me like that and why did I have to fall for it?

I could feel that my face was red and looking at his big grin made everything so much worse. All I could do was try to calm myself down.

What could I do though? He did this in front of everyone and they didn't say a word. What happened to the people who feared me? I know it wasn't them, but shouldn't they be afraid of me?

"Well, aren't you two getting along well?" Queen Widow said, smiling at the both of us.

Sirius spoke and said, "She's not bad," smirking as if he's going to have fun messing with me.

"Son— how about you take her to the caves and tell her why she's possibly here," King Shadow said, leaving me a little worried.

"The caves—?"

CHAPTER 8

Sirius and I entered the caves.

The cave was dark, and the sound of silence was scary. Luckily, we had a flashlight to help us see.

But as we got further into the cave a glow shined brightly. "We're almost there," he spoke.

Once we arrived, I found myself amazed.

This cave had writing I didn't understand and pictures on the wall that looked like history.

"What is all of this?"

I walked to the wall, looking at the pictures closely. Suddenly, Sirius grabbed my wrist and pinned me roughly against the wall.

I didn't know what was happening at that moment nor did I understand what his deal was. I had to admit that everything he did, or said was exciting to me.

"This is the history of No Eyes— those people on the wall are those who were like us, but since you are here, it changes things." He said, getting closer and closer to me.

"What do you mean? I'm not sure I understand you."

"I mean what they said about someone going to sleep and waking up in our world, if they are truly one of us.

Especially, if they are the chosen one."

A slight blush appeared on my cheeks from him staring into my eyes.

"Are you saying that I'm the chosen one? If so, why me and how?"

"Darling, you're in my world right now and tomorrow if you fall asleep ending up in my world again, we'll just say you are the chosen one -- the chosen one to save the world."

I laughed. "Me? Save the world?"

"Everyone on this wall died saving this world, but for the first time in forever we have a button eye who is chosen. Maybe there's something about you that will make you the hero of this story."

"I'm confused."

"You're really clueless, aren't you?" He backed away from me looking annoyed.

"I'm not clueless; I just want to make sure I understand correctly," I said, feeling my eyes become heavy while rubbing them.

"Looks like sleeping beauty is waking up," he smirked.
"No... I need..."

*I couldn't finish my sentence, but before everything went black as he said, "You'll understand soon, but in the meantime it's time for you to wake up, my **princess.**"*

CHAPTER 9

His voice was so calm and attractive that I didn't even want to wake up.

I started to hear someone yelling my name.

When I woke up in my bed, it was surprising to me -- confusing at that.

Was it all a dream? I thought to myself, getting out of bed and walking into the kitchen to see my father sitting at the table, looking upset as if I did something wrong.

"Yes?"

"When I call you, you need to come as soon as possible, not take your time. Do you understand?"

He looked furious at me, but I wasn't the one at fault. "Yes, I understand."

"Now, hurry up and make some breakfast. I have a busy schedule today and I don't want to deal with an annoying brat like you."

I stood there staring at him, wondering why I let this man walk all over me. That is until he yelled at me-

"HEY! DO WHAT YOU'RE TOLD NOW!"

"Sorry... Right away."

I began making breakfast for him as quickly as possible. When I was done making his breakfast, he ate it and left. Looking outside the window, he was talking to someone who I couldn't see clearly through the shadows, but who cares. That wasn't important.

It made me happy he was gone, so I decided to make myself some food that would be way better than I had given him. Then I got dressed to see my friends.

"Hey, Chrysan," Blossom said, coming up to hug me. "Hey."

"Are you okay?" Nova asked. She looked concerned. Wait, let's take a pause really quick just so you readers, know Nova is the true friend and Blossom is the fake one. No need to get into too many details yet.

"I'm fine, but the craziest thing happened last night and I don't know if it was real or not."

"What do you mean?" they both asked curiously. "I saw them... The ones with no eyes."

Blossom and Nova were shocked.

"You saw them? When? How? Wait, is it true that if you're the chosen one you'll wake up in their world?"

"Last night when I went to sleep, I woke up in their world, but this morning, I woke up in my bed like nothing happened.

I'm confused... I'm not even sure if that guy I met was real."

"A guy?" Nova questioned.

"Yes... a guy-" I started to say, looking up quickly at the two of them who were grinning widely.

"Tell us about him," Blossom said, smiling. I started blushing just thinking about Sirius.

"Well... he's cute, but he has the worst personality. He was so rude to me and he did call me names a lot, which was embarrassing.

He even teased me a couple of times." "Teased?" Nova questioned.

"He, umm, lifted up my chin like he was about to kiss me and pinned me against the wall." I said, blushing.

Both screamed loudly with excitement and hugged me tightly. "I think this guy has an interest in you, Chrysan," Nova said, still excited.

"I bet you guys would be so cute together, but what's wrong?" Blossom asked as she looked at me, concerned. "What if I don't see him again? What if I'm not the chosen one?"

I looked sad that I may not be able to see the ones with No Eyes ever again.

CHAPTER 10

Nova and Blossom looked at each other concerned.

"Oh... Chrysan you shouldn't say that. I mean you don't know if you're the chosen one or not, but if you are— you can see them again."

Blossom held my hand, staring into my eyes trying to tell me everything would be alright.

"I have an idea. What if you try to go to sleep right now?" Nova suggested.

"What?"

"Me and Blossom can tell you what happens when you go to sleep and see if your body is here when you're in the No Eyes world."

"And what if her body isn't here, who will wake her up?" Blossom questioned.

"Hopefully, someone there wakes her up, so you can come back. What do you say, shall we try it out? "Nova asked.

"Let's give it a shot," I said, lying on the grass, starting to close my eyes.

BUTTON EYES, NO EYES

"No matter what happens over here, we will be here until you wake up," Nova said.

In a matter of seconds— I fell asleep just like last night, what happened next made me one of the happiest girls alive.

I woke up in the No Eyes world once again, this time in a new location. It looked like someone was having a campfire.

That was correct -- Sirius and his friends were.

I walked over there and everyone turned to look at me. "The princess has gone to sleep again?" Sirius spoke. He was happy to see me.

Not only that, but his friends were acting as if they knew me already.

I'm not sure why, but I felt someone's eyes watching me in the shadows that wasn't any of his friends, but I couldn't let that bother me.

"Were you guys playing a game?" I asked.

Each of them nodded their heads. One of Sirius's friends asked if I wanted to play and I responded back saying yes to the game without knowing the rules.

***"Button Eyes or No Eyes?"** Sirius asked.*

I was confused as to why he was asking me that so randomly.

Shouldn't I learn how the game works first? Was it part of the game to not know about it, or just something else?
"No Eyes."

I'm not sure why, but when those two words came out of my mouth, Sirius' friends started smirking at each other.

Sirius, on the other hand, stood up and walked towards me.

My heart was beating so fast as he walked closer to me, but the most surprising and flustering moment was when he lifted my chin up and asked.

"Are you sure you want to pick No

Eyes?" "Yes."

Sirius then leaned in and kissed me on the lips.

The kiss was gentle and soft. It gave me butterflies, but the question is why he did this— Was it because I chose the No Eyes?

What would happen if I chose Button Eyes?

When he broke the kiss, he and his friends looked really concerned.

At first, I didn't know why they looked so concerned, but when touching my face, I felt tears coming down.

There was something weird about my tears being here compared to my own world.

My left eye was crying tears of green, and my right was crying tears of black. There was a moment of silence until Sirius broke it by saying—

"A black tear."

CHAPTER 11

Sirius asked me a question. "How can you possibly have a black tear?"

His friends were whispering to each other, looking creeped out. I couldn't stand there while they talked about me, so I ran away from them.

To my surprise, Sirius left his friends and ran after me. "Stop running," he said, trying to catch up to me.

He grabbed my waist and held me close to him, whispering into my ear.

"Chrysan, please no more running."

"Are you going to judge me just like your friends?"

"No."

Looking at his expression, I could tell he was serious about not judging me.

"Why not?"

"Why would I judge you, little bunny?"

I looked up at Sirius and he was staring into my eyes more deeply than ever. "Because my tears are different and I don't know why" I said, while my voice was cracking.

"It's not your fault and I don't blame you for not knowing why your tears are like this. I was just surprised, because I had never seen anything like that."

"I'm sorry."

I couldn't hold my tears back and started crying. Sirius wiped my green and black tears away.

"Don't worry, everything will be okay" he said, softly.

"Will it really b-" I started to say, but I started dozing off again like the first time.

I knew that would mean I was waking up again.

"Listen to me, since you're about to leave my world again, just know you can come back whenever. You are the chosen one, okay?"

Nodding my head before falling asleep, I woke up to my friends looking worried. "Finally, you came back."

"Was my body still here and what's wrong?"

"No, when you went to the No Eyes world your body went with it too. Umm, you should hurry home now," Nova said.

There was confusion about why I should, but the looks on their faces made me realize that it had something to do with my father and if I didn't hurry back, I would be in big trouble.

I ran back to the house, realizing it was too late. I slowly opened the front door and closed it quietly, but suddenly the lights came on. "Where were you?" he asked.

I didn't turn around to face him until he yelled at me, which left me no choice but to face him.

"WHERE WERE YOU!?"

"With Blossom and Nova." "You know you're late?"

"Yes, and I'm sorry. I tried to get here as fast as I could, but it seems that didn't happen."

He stood up from his chair and the unthinkable happened—

CHAPTER 12

My father slapped me across the room and grabbed a knife from the kitchen.

"Now what should I do about you, brat?" "Please... I'm sorry."

My voice started to crack. What was about to happen was going to be painful and there was nothing that could be done to fix it.

"Ah, I know exactly what I should do."

He walked towards me and made sure that I wouldn't be able to run.

He stabbed my hand with the knife and that caused me to scream and cry loudly. I knew that everyone who lived around here would be able to hear it, but would they care? No.

Not in the least. This man started laughing like he enjoyed seeing me in pain.

Grayson was truly crazy.

I couldn't help wondering why this man was my father out of all people. After stabbing my hand, he kept hitting and beating me with anything hard he could find in the house.

Hurting me was fun for him and when he left the house again, he left me to bleed out. There was blood around me, I was covered in bruises and cuts.

Blood was everywhere and on everything. I took the knife out of my hand, which made my hand bleed even more.

Then I walked towards the bathroom.

However, the bathroom door wasn't opening, meaning he had locked it.

I tried opening a couple of doors in the house, but the only door that was open was my bedroom door.

I quickly went into my room and locked it.

I needed to go to sleep, so Sirius could give me some treatment, but instead of going to sleep, I passed out. "She's been out for a couple of hours now, Father." "She'll be okay, son."

Waking up, there were voices that sounded familiar to me. "She is waking up…"

I looked around and saw Sirius, the queen and the king. "Where am I?"

"You're in our hospital, dear." *the queen said, gently smiling at me.*

"How long was I passed out?"

"A couple of hours," *King Shadow said.*

"What? Wait, it's not nighttime here, is it?" I worriedly spoke.

"No... It's not, but what happened to you, Chrysan? Who did this to you?" Sirius asked.

I started to cry and said "My father—"

Sirius became angry and he punched the wall. His mother and father didn't try to calm him down.

Instead, a man, who looked like a guard, entered the room, trying to calm him down, but it didn't work.

Whoever this was, for some reason, I couldn't help but look at him.

He reminded me of myself, but an older male version.

My attention was quickly lost when Widow

spoke. "Dear, how long has he been doing this to you? Please be honest with me."

"Since I was a little girl- after my mother passed, he started abusing me whenever he pleased, or if I messed up one little thing."

I wiped my tears, trying to stay strong.

"WHY HAVEN'T YOU TOLD ANYONE CHRYSAN!?"

Sirius yelled, causing me to start crying again. "SIRIUS! ENOUGH, SON!" Shadow spoke. "DON'T TELL ME WHAT TO DO!"

They were arguing back and forth.

I'm not sure who could truly handle any of this, but it wasn't me.

"BOTH OF YOU, STOP!" I yelled.

CHAPTER 13

Both turned to look at me with a shocked expression on their faces.

"I'm sorry... I didn't mean to yell, but please, there's no need to start an argument because of me."

I looked at Sirius and said, "I haven't told anyone, because that could cause the people I care about to get hurt, or I could tell the wrong person, which would be endangering myself."

"I'm sorry— I didn't know," Sirius said feeling bad.

"Dear– I wish there was a way we could keep you here, so you wouldn't have to go through that again" he said, walking towards me.

Everyone in the room looked down, including myself.

"Let's not worry about that right now. Are you hungry?" Sirius asked.

I nodded my head yes and before I knew it, I was checked out of the hospital, walking with Sirius.

It was just the two of us, but it was quiet. I could tell he was still angry from what I told him.

"You think I'm still angry, don't you?" he asked, as he stopped walking and grabbed my hand.

"I do."

"Well, to tell you the truth, I'm more worried about you than angry."

"Why would you worry about me? You know nothing about me. I haven't been in your world long enough."

He cut me off by kissing me. I pushed him away and touched my lips with my finger.

"Stop trying to kiss me. I am nothing to you and you are nothing to me."

"Then, why did you cry when I kissed you the first time?"
"I don't— I don't know, okay?"

"That's more of a reason to let me kiss you," he said, trying to kiss me once again, but I blocked it.

"I told you to stop. I have no feelings for you and you have no feelings for me.

We're not playing whatever game right now that you and your friends played— that I didn't know how to play since no explanation of the rules were told."

"I think it's better if you don't know the rules of the game that way, I can have my fun with you."

He smirked.

"I am who I am and you need to understand that. I have only been here for a short amount of time and now suddenly you want to kiss me?

Don't make me laugh, because you can't be that dumb to kiss a girl like me."

Sirius sat down near a tree and I followed right behind him, sitting down too.

"At first, I just wanted to mess around with you, but kissing you changed that. I felt connected to you in a way." "Connected? You sound crazy."

"I'm not crazy. I feel like you understand my people and it's like you're one of us."

"I don't really understand your people. Sirius, whatever you may think is completely wrong."

"Maybe it could just be me, but that's why I may be interested in you more than you think. I'll back off."

Sirius got up and gave me a signal to follow him, so we could eat.

When I got up to walked towards him someone bumped into me, but when I tried to say sorry, but he was already gone.

That was weird, but whatever. I didn't know why, but talking about the kiss for some reason made me want to kiss him again.

I couldn't let that happen, because what if I was to fall in love with him? Or would that really be a bad thing to love him?

CHAPTER 14

Sirius and I started eating together at the table. "The food here is so good," I said, continuing to eat.

Sirius didn't say anything, but he smiled at me while eating his food.

For a moment I stopped eating, which kind of concerned Sirius. "What's wrong?"

"When my father was abusing me, my tears weren't different colors, but they were green."

"Continue."

"It's weird. When I'm here, my tears are two different colors, but for some reason in my world they only show one."

"Sounds like you're being protected by the hidden truth," he laughed.

Actually, what he joked about made me think he could be on to something.

I didn't want to worry about it or tell him, because he might start to believe my mind was going crazy inside.

I'll just possibly do my own research, whenever I have the time which I am hoping–

My forgetfulness doesn't stop me.

Once he finished eating, we walked around. He showed me some of his favorite places.

Taking a walk with him, I learned more about him and his people, which made me wonder why I couldn't be one of them.

You know I'm not able to wish for whom I was born from or what species, creature, or person should be me.

Some part of me feels like I belong here. "This place-"

"Did it catch your eye? That's the-"

"Sea," *I said, cutting Sirius off and finishing his sentence.* "You know about the sea?" *he asked, giving a confused expression.*

I know you're probably wondering why he would be confused about me knowing about the sea-

Well in my world, we have no sea, no ocean, no lake, and no water.

We don't have any books about them either.

"It's like I've been here before," *I said, staring deep into the sea.*

"That's not possible." "Why not?" *I asked.*

"Well because the sea can only be found here, so you couldn't possibly have seen it."

I accidently yelled at him, and said, "I'M TELLING YOU I HAVE BEEN HERE BEFORE!"

"There's no need to raise your voice, Chrysan."

"Sorry."

"Look- it's not that I don't want to believe you, but it's not possible, okay?"

"Leave."

"What?"

"I said LEAVE!"

Sirius looked sad and walked away. When he left, I ran towards the sea.

CHAPTER 15

I ran and ran, but getting closer caused me to stop. There was no fear in me, but only hesitation. Should I put my feet in the water? No, what if it's too deep underneath? Sirius isn't here, so if I were to drown, who would save me? Turning away from the sea, I heard a sound. It was the sound of a whale, that was trying to speak to me. I turned around, but there was no sign of a whale and the sound disappeared without a trace. I took my shoes off and went into the water, but before I knew it, I was deep underwater. I would have thought this was the end of me, knowing I wasn't able to swim, but someone saved me.

*Losing air, I was suddenly pulled up to the surface and that's when I saw **HIM**.*

It was a boy and he looked like a whale, just more human- like.

He was cute. The guy made a noise, I didn't understand. He came closer to me and grabbed my hand."

"Hello," he said, still holding my hand.

"You speak my language?" "Now I do."

"What do you mean now you do?" I asked, looking into his eyes.

"I was talking to you in a language you didn't understand, so grabbing your hand helped me to understand you. In other words, just simple magic does the trick."

"I see, but who are you?"

"I'm Shane, a humpback whale mermaid. I live here in the sea."

"Nice to meet you, Shane. "I'm-" I started to say, but he cut me off and let go of my hand.

"Chrysan, I know your name."

"How could you know my name?"

"This isn't the first time we met, you know. Don't tell me you forgot about me all these years," he laughed.

The truth was, I didn't know who he was, but if he knew me that just proved my point in my being here before.

"I don't remember you, I'm sorry."

"Yako s'ti."

My eyes widened, but in a blink of an eye, my body was back in my own bed again. I was confused by the words

he said, wondering why the language sounded so familiar to me in a way.

"Breathe, Chrysan," I told myself.

Getting up and going to the library, I figured maybe there could be information on the language and more about who I am.

None of this made any sense, but I bet if my mom was here she could figure it out.

As I walked to the library, I enjoyed the beautiful nature. Pain appeared in my chest, making me feel the tears coming down my face.

I was having a breakdown, a panic attack and no one was around to calm me down. I missed my mother so much and I hated being abused by my father all the time.

Love was a real pain in my eyes. I wanted everything to get better now.

Somehow. Some way.

*I wish that my life would be **different**.*

CHAPTER 16

A voice called my name, telling me everything would be okay. I thought maybe insanity went through my head, because there was a vision in my eyes from a long time ago.

It looked like the four-year-old me and another kid.

I couldn't see the kid's face, but he looked like he was trying to say something, but who was to know.

"Hturt ehe erbmemerr," *he said.*

I realized the language was the same language Shane spoke.

I wonder how Shane and this boy from my vision could know this language. It was not the same, because Shane lived in the sea and whoever this kid was had two feet.

What was weird was, blinking my eyes caused me to go back to the No Eyes world. It was strange since I didn't go to sleep, but blinked. However, it was different this time.

In their world, I was in the library. Sirius wasn't around, nor was the queen, king, not even Shane.

There was only me, who was left alone and it hurt so much.

All I did was focus on searching for any leads there was a reason for being here.

I Looked, read, and continued on, but there was nothing.

Everything at this point seemed so confusing and so pointless. I couldn't even stand it anymore.

"Lalala I can't hear you."

"Who said that?" I said, looking back and forth, trying to see who was in here with me.

"Chrysan, wait for me."

The kid who said my name sounded like the same voice I heard earlier, but where was it coming from?

There was no vision like before, but at the corner of my eye, I saw a bright glow. "A book?"

I grabbed a ladder to climb to the top to reach it. The book came closer to me.

The glow was simply disappearing. I reached for the book and opened it.

The weird thing was the book, without warning, sucked me inside. It seemed as if I was inside the same library, but it looked older.

"Chrysan." "Yes?"

When I turned around, there was little me talking to a boy, whose face I still couldn't see.

"I like you," he spoke.

"I like you, too.," she smiled.

The boy's expression looked so serious, even if I couldn't see him.

"No! I mean I like you a lot, Chrysan."

If I'm being honest, the look on his face as he said that, caused me to have the same reaction as hers.

CHAPTER 17

"Wait... what?"

"How do you feel about me?" "I like you a lot, too."

She and the boy stared into each other's eyes. He held her hand. "Then we can start dating?"

"Sorry, but there's no way we could possibly be together."

He removed his hand from mine and took a step back away from me.

"It's because we're different, isn't it?" "You know we can't be together—"

He became angry and heartbroken. I felt his pain, but why did it seem like the younger me didn't feel it? Or maybe she did, but didn't show it at the time.

"You say this to everyone, it's always you can't be with them, but you won't say why. I'm just tired of it now."

"You wouldn't understand."

"TELL ME WHY! I don't understand."

"Because you're not me."

"Excuse me?"

"YOU'RE NOT ME!" she yelled.

What was confusing was that after so many years, I was only just starting to remember things I didn't know before.

I was lost in thought, when the page turned into a book and appeared in the house that seemed familiar to me.

"WHY DO YOU KEEP RUNNING AWAY FROM ME?!"

"I DON'T WANT YOU TO TOUCH ME, CHRYSAN!"

"WHY NOT?! TELL ME NOW!"

The yelling and the screaming hurt my heart so badly, even though I couldn't see who this person was.

Where was I, why I kept wondering? I just wanted to remember everything.

The younger me wasn't four anymore, but she looked twelve to me and if she was, this didn't happen long ago. "Chrysan, stop please."

His voice softened.

"YOU CAN'T TELL ME TO STOP! WHY TELL ME NOW?"

"I DON'T WANT TO HURT YOU, CHRYSAN! WHY DON'T YOU UNDERSTAND THAT!

I AM A MONSTER.

You were right, we don't belong together, we can't be together, we are just too different."

"I never said we didn't belong together. I did say, we can't be together though.

However, I want you more than anything in the world, monster or not."

"Why?" he said, hearing his voice breaking. He was about to start crying.

*"Because **I love you**."*

Tears fell down my face, but I didn't understand why.

"You can't love someone, if everything will end before it even begins."

CHAPTER 18

She started crying as well, it wasn't just me. We both felt the pain. "We can still try."

"No."

"Why? You can't tell me it's because of that. You must give me a real reason."

"I don't love you" he said, looking away from me.

He looked back at me once more to see my expression.

"What?"

"You heard me."

I yelled at him, "YOU ARE A LIAR!"

"Why would I lie? I don't want you, nor do I love you, Chrysan. I want you gone, away from my life."

"You don't actually mean that."

I reached my hand out towards the younger me and the boy, but before I could, the page turned once again.

This time, it was night and the sound of crying pierced the air. "Do you really have to leave now?" she asked, looking concerned.

"I don't want to leave, but I need to." "Why won't you tell me why?"

"It would hurt me as much as it would hurt you."

"I won't fall in love with anyone else, I will only love you."

"No."

"No?"

"You will love someone else, trust me on that."

"No! I won't."

"You won't remember meeting me once I leave, that's part of what I let my parents do to me."

"I don't understand what you're saying."

"Don't worry about it, just come here."

She walked over to him, and he kissed her on the lips. The kiss seemed long, but it felt as if I was being kissed at this moment.

After our long kiss, he broke it and I blushed. "The kiss was a goodbye kiss, wasn't it?"

"For right now, my love, yes it is a goodbye kiss", as he kissed my hand and slowly backed away.

"You'll always know where to find me, until then remember the whole truth."

CHAPTER 19

I woke up in my bed, sweating a lot.

I decided to take a shower before going back to sleep, since it would seem whatever happened made time go faster. There was a lot on my mind, wondering what I saw and heard.

Ever since I arrived at the No Eyes world, my life has been changing each day.

Was what I saw all a dream, or was it reality?

The truth needed to stand out in the light.

I went to sleep once again, feeling lost and blinded, because the darkness of the night was getting to me, wondering in my dreams, ***Why Me****?*

CHAPTER 20

The next day, Blossom walked towards me with a happy expression, as she said hi to me. I haven't seen Blossom, or Nova for a while, but it was just Blossom.

"Hey, Blossom. Where is Nova? She's not with you today?"

"I haven't seen her around actually." *Blossom's face expression changed from happiness to worry.*

"What do you mean?"

"I tried to visit her yesterday, but her parents wouldn't allow me. Who knows? maybe she's dead," *she laughed.*

It's funny, because Blossom was always the fake friend in my eyes, but we still hung around her.

"Do you think she's okay?"

"I hope so, because I'm really concerned, Chrysan. What if something happened to her and her parents don't want us to know?"

Why did this girl have to pretend like she cared about us when she really didn't?

"How about we go there now?"

"Are you sure? I mean, what if her parents are home?"

"Her parents should be at work at this time."

Blossom took a deep breath and nodded her head yes. We both headed towards Nova's house, but what we heard next was shocking and heartbreaking. "We finished the job, sir."

"You killed her?"

"Yes. Nova is dead and her body is hidden."

"Good."

"What happens if Blossom and Chrysan find out that their best friend is dead?

What will you do then? Will you kill them too?"

"As long as they both don't get in the way of my plans, everything will be fine," *a strange unfamiliar voice spoke to them.*

"What did my daughter Nova find out? I mean you made me kill her so the least you could do is tell me what she found out."

"She found out the truth about how Chrysan's whole life is a lie," *he spoke.*

Who was this person? This conversation made me sick to my stomach.

I couldn't listen any further.

"Blossom let's go," I said, holding back my tears, so we wouldn't get caught.

Once we were further away, I broke into tears. Blossom hugged me tightly and told me everything would be okay.

I just knew that if I had gotten a quick look at who had done this, he could be found, but my heart was too broken. "Is this my fault?"

"NO, OF COURSE NOT!" she yelled, staring me in the eyes.

"Then, why did this happen?"

"It only happened, because people don't care about anyone, but themselves.

Trust me this is not your fault, Chrysan." "I feel like it's my fault, Blossom."

She watched me cry, saying this was my fault (on repeat) that Nova died.

Do I blame myself? I do. Why?

Whoever the mastermind was, my father had to be involved in Nova's death.

CHAPTER 21

I wish Nova was here or given us a sign about what she had found out.

Did my life being a lie involve the death of my mother?

"Do you feel better now, Chrysan?" Blossom asked.

I stood up and said, "I want to find out about my life and this plan they spoke of."

"It could be dangerous."

"I know, but who's to say that I couldn't get help?"

"You mean--"

I smiled and nodded yes.

"The No Eyes world."

The first person I could think of to ask for help was Sirius.

We haven't spoken since I told him to leave when we were near the sea that day.

I feel bad for not talking to him since then. I hope he's okay and hasn't been worried about me. Thinking that he'd be worried about me was foolish of me.

"Sirius."

I called out his name.

He turned his head towards me with a shocked expression.

"Chrysan," *he spoke, leaving me standing there, looking at the girl in front of him.*

Why did I care so much if he was with another girl? "Who is she?" I asked as tears started to flow.

"Why did you come back, Chrysan?" he spoke angrily at me.

"WHY DID I COME BACK? ARE YOU SERIOUS, SIRIUS?"

Sirius walked towards me and grabbed my wrist roughly. We walked away together and once we were alone, he removed his grip off my wrist. "You should have never come back."

"I'm allowed to come back whenever I want, you don't CONTROL me, Sirius."

"I DO CONTROL YOU."

"No."

"I'M THE PRINCE OF THE NO EYES WORLD! I'M NOT YOUR FRIEND! I AM NOTHING TO YOU, BUT YOUR SOON-TO-BE KING."

My eyes widened, because he had changed so much since the last time I saw him and not in a good way.

I only wanted to say sorry to him about what happened that day, but there was change of plan.

I couldn't ask for his help anymore, because he is the only son, soon to be king.

"You're not the same person I knew."

Sirius gave me a cold look and I went down on my knees, avoiding eye contact with him, by putting my head down on the ground.

"I was out of line by calling you a name, but you are a prince, which are two different things. I understand now."

"Now you know your place."

I stood up still avoiding eye contact with him.

"Is that girl you were kissing your girlfriend?"

"She'll be the next queen."

"You are getting married to her? Why?"

"Because I love her."

CHAPTER 22

My heart broke and I didn't understand why.

I barely knew the guy, but felt like he and I knew each other for a whole lifetime.

"You-you lo-love her?"

"Why hesitate, it's not like I ever loved you."

Those words crushed my heart into a million pieces, and the only person to possibly blame was myself.

"I see."

I could hear Sirius' footsteps walking away, then they stopped. I figured he was gone, but he wasn't, because he turned around and walked back towards me.

He lifted my chin up and stared into my eyes. "What are you doing?" I asked.

"You don't need to care about what happened between me and you at the sea that day."

"But-"

"You don't belong to me, and you never did. I lost that battle a long time ago."

"What?"

Whatever Sirius was talking about, it could be what was happening to me now, with my whole life being a lie.

Everything was confusing and didn't make sense anymore.

"You love someone else, not me."

"How can I love someone else? Are you talking about the guy from the sea because"?

"I'm not talking about him."

He was confusing me so much, I didn't understand what he was saying.

"Who are you talking about?"

"The guy in your visions."

My facial expression changed from confusion to shock. I couldn't believe what was just said.

Sirius knew about the visions.

How? He shouldn't even know about that. I was the only one who could see those visions, right?

Unless—

"HOW DO YOU KNOW THAT? ARE YOU WATCHING ME OR USING SOME SORT OF

MAGIC? NO, WHAT IS IT YOU KNOW, SIRIUS, THAT YOU'RE NOT TELLING ME?!"

"Gnihtyna wonk t'nod I," he said, backing away from me slowly. I looked down at the ground still shocked about what was happening.

The language. "How do you know-" I said, lifting my head, but he was gone.

Sirius did know something, but wasn't trying to tell me. How do I know? Because the language he spoke was the same language I heard more than once.

"What is happening?"

CHAPTER 23

Returning home, I told Blossom everything that happened. She couldn't help wondering when Sirius had gotten a girlfriend. He didn't even act like he had an interest in me, but it seemed he didn't have any interest at all.

"Isn't that a little bit too early to be moving on?" She asked, I replied to her saying, "He said that I belonged to someone else, but I didn't know who."

"Why would he say that?"

"I'm not sure, but I had visions about a guy I kissed when I was younger, but I wasn't able to see his face."

"Your life seems to be falling apart..."

"I know and I hate it."

"My whole life is a lie, it makes me really want to know the truth."

"I wish I could help you find the truth, but I can't." 'Why not?" I turned to her.

"I can't tell you."

"Did my father threaten you?"

"No."

She looked afraid, that I knew that he had threatened her, but she just didn't want to tell me.

Why would he threaten her about the truth? What did he know?

"HE THREATENED YOU BLOSSOM, WHEN?!"

"A while ago, but I just didn't tell you."

I was very upset that I walked away from Blossom and went home only to find my father sitting on the couch.

He had weapons everywhere and it made me scared of what might happen next.

"Welcome home," he said, grinning. "Hi."

"How was your day? I made dinner." "Umm, it was fine."

I slowly sat down at the table. I couldn't help, but wonder why he was being a little bit normal, by asking me how my day was. It was weird, but I had a feeling he asked, because he didn't want me to know that he was part of the reason why blossom didn't tell me.

Maybe it was the fact that Nova was dead and that he had threatened Blossom.

"Why are you being so nice to me?"

"I can't be nice to my daughter?"

"It's not that, but you are always hurting me."

"I'm sorry about that. I never meant to hurt you, but I want all that to change."

"What do you mean?"

"No more secrets between us anymore, okay?"

"You mean--"

"I'll tell you all my secrets and everything you want to know."

CHAPTER 24

I was shocked to hear those words from him, but I just had a feeling he was lying to me. "Talk then…"

"I told Nova's parents to kill her and I threatened Blossom."

It was hard to believe that he was the one giving orders for her to die, when the person who was talking to Nova's parents wasn't him.

Since that was the cause, I played along, pretending to be shocked.

"Why?" I asked.

"Your friend Nova didn't know how to stay in her place and stay out of my business.

Blossom did nothing, but I had to threaten her, so she wouldn't be like Nova."

"BUT YOU DIDN'T HAVE TO KILL NOVA," I yelled,

standing up from my chair, causing it to fall back.

"Don't raise your voice at me, Chrysan."

"You cannot tell me what to do…"

"Chrysan, I want you to help me with my plan."

"What?"

"I hurt you enough and you can use that pain for my plan."

"Excuse me?"

My father stood up and looked at me with intense in his eyes and said, "I'll give you a choice to either join me in this plan, or I won't be afraid to hurt you, or anyone you care about."

I couldn't believe he was threatening me.

I could join his plan and figure out why I'm the chosen one to save the world. Even find out the truth!

Now that I think about it, I haven't said anything about me being the chosen one in so long, until now.

"I'll join you in your plan, but you have to tell me everything about this plan."

"I don't know if I can trust you right now. You're hiding something."

"If you don't trust me, I'm not going to be part of this."

"You'll change your mind soon enough," he laughed and my father got up and left the house. I just knew I needed to find out what Nova found out before she was killed, other than how my mother died.

She possibly found out more than what was said. Maybe there was some sort of message she left for me and Blossom. Little did I know, Nova had left many messages for us, but we just had to play a little game to find them.

CHAPTER 25

The first message Nova left was an item in my room. It was a rock, but I remember seeing this rock, maybe near a spot Blossom, Nova and I loved to throw rocks. Then, it hit me.

The spot was near an abandoned house, where we all threw rocks for fun.

I decided to go with Blossom to that spot, but we would have to be very careful.

Later

"Are you sure there's a clue here?"

"There was a rock in my room and how else would it have gotten there?"

"Maybe your father?"

"I don't think he's ever been in my room before, so it couldn't possibly be him."

"Are you sure about that?"

"What do you mean?"

"He started being nice to you and wants you to join him for his plan, but won't tell you what it is.

Do you think he's not capable of doing this?"

"Okay, you have a point."

"Anything is possible."

"Yes, I know! Let's see what we can find here. If we don't find anything, we can go home." Blossom and I kept looking for messages around the house, clues that Nova may have left for us, but nothing was there.

"There is nothing here, Chrysan, let's go."

"You can go without me, I'm going to stay and keep looking."

"I shouldn't leave you alone here, it's not safe." "It's fine. Just go!"

Blossom left, while I kept looking, but for some reason, someone was watching me. At least that was what it felt like.

"Chrysan."

A voice called, startling me!

I was in an abandoned house. "Do you see, Chrysan?"

I looked at the wall and I saw these drawings that weren't here before, when Blossom was here.

It was almost like it was-

"Hidden."

CHAPTER 26

Why was it hidden? Could I be the only one who is able to see these images?

Why do these images show my childhood?

"Is everything I know a lie?" I said, loudly to myself.

"Yes."

Although, it was already told to me, I didn't know the truth.

"If it's a lie, I want to know the truth NOW!"

"You can't."

I'm not sure I understand, but the voice I heard was everywhere, which made my head spin.

"Why not?"

"You must wait until the time is right, my honey."

"What does that mean?"

"The day you decide you want to save the world will be the day the truth will come to light."

"I want to stop my father from his bad doings, it could the light to my answers."

"I don't mean, just your father. You will save your world and other worlds that will soon come to face danger."

"W-h-a-t."

*SUDDENLY, everything went **black!***

CHAPTER 27

Being in darkness is scary, especially when you hear a voice asking you if you're okay and you don't know who said it.

"Who said?" I started to ask, continuing to open my eyes only to see myself under water.

I looked around to see who was talking while holding my breath.

I finally saw the person, it was Shane. He grabbed my hand and he took me somewhere.

"Now breathe," he said as we arrived at some island. "Shane, since when can you walk? You are a sea creature."

"I only have legs for a limited time, but we need to hurry before we wake this island up."

"What do you mean?" I asked as I followed him.

"You are wondering what's going on, right?"

"Wait, you know the truth?"

"I do but—"

"You can't tell me, can you?"

"I'm sorry, but there are many people close to you who know the truth, even if it doesn't seem like you're that close to them."

"Almost like the ones you least expect..." Shane turned his face towards me and smiled.

"We're here."

"What is this place?"

"It's the memory of water. Once you go in, look deep into the water and a memory will appear.

I'm not sure what memory it will give you, but whatever memory it does show, just know that it is part of your past."

I nodded my head and entered.

The place was so beautiful and the water was glowing like diamonds. I slowly got on my knees and looked into the water.

CHAPTER 28

Flashback

"Chrysan, are you listening?"

"Huh? I'm sorry, I wasn't listening."

"What's going on with you?"

"Nothing."

"Come here."

He hugged me closely causing me to blush. "You're embarrassing me, Lee."

"I can't help that you're cute."

"Are you sure about this?"

"You wanted to see my world, so I'm showing you."

"What will they think when they see me?"

"Who cares! I want you to see how I see my world love and that's all that matters."

A few hours later things between me and Lee got a little intense.

We were walking back to the house and I tried to get him to talk. "Lee, talk to me."

He just kept ignoring me, but he gave me this scary look. However, he finally spoke to me.

"Taking you here was a mistake," he said as he stopped walking.

"What? No, it was a great idea," I said smiling, but that was my worst mistake.

Everything we went past was dying or getting destroyed. I figured it had to do with Lee's curse, but I didn't want to say anything to him.

"We should have broken up a long time ago."

I stared at Lee in fear, because why would he ever say that to me of all people.

He didn't even look me in the eye when he spoke, so he couldn't have meant those words.

"Lee…I'm--"

"Don't waste your time saying sorry."

"But…"

"I'm going to take you back to your world. You can't stay here anymore, Chrysan."

Lee looked back and saw all the damage he had done without even noticing.

"I'm a monster."

CHAPTER 29

Lee turned back to look at me and I felt afraid of him. His eyes were filled with evil. He looked ready to murder me and anyone who gets in his way,

"Are you okay? You look like you're about to murder someone," I spoke.

Suddenly, he tried to attack me, but somehow I was teleported somewhere else. Tears fell from my face, because the man that I loved was turning into a monster.

No, he was one.

Why did he have to be one out of everyone in the world? "Glad I was able to save you before he hurt you."

I looked up and saw Sirius. "Thank you."

Sirius leaned down and wiped my tears away as I continued to cry.

"You have to stop crying."

"I can't."

I tried wiping my tears away, but the tears kept coming.

"I don't understand why you two keep trying to make things work. You both are different."

"I know, he's a monster and you're you."

"You don't understand what it's like to be me."

"That may be true princess, but at the same time, I do." *Sirius telling me that he understood me made me snap, because he didn't see what I saw. Sirius and I were arguing nonstop.*

"YOU DON'T SEE ME! HOW CAN YOU WHEN YOU HAVE NO EYES TO SEE WHAT I SEE?!"

Sirius grabs my hand and stares deep into my eyes.

"I see your eyes, I see your color, I see your beauty, I see your smile, I see your personality, but most of all, I still see you."

He didn't yell at me when he said those words, but I knew he meant every word.

"I know you see me," *I quietly said, looking deep into his eyes.*

"So let me love you."

"I will not stop you from loving me, but I can't return the feelings you have for me. I'm in love with Lee and you already know that."

"He'll break your heart in the end, so you sure you want to love him?"

"He won't break my heart. I am confident he will always love me, no matter what we go through."

I truly did love Lee with all my heart, even if he was a monster. Even if he did try to hurt me early by accident, it was not his fault.

He didn't ask to be a monster.

CHAPTER 30

Sirius looked at me like I had made a big mistake, but who cares. He can find someone else to love.

I went to look for Lee, whom I haven't seen in a couple of hours.

When I found him, he was sitting down, looking sad and lonely. "Can we talk?" I asked, sitting next to him.

"Talk."

"I'm sorry taking me here was a mistake." Lee turned to face me, leaning closer to me.

"It wasn't a mistake. I was afraid you would get hurt, because they tried to attack you earlier." His voice softened.

"Lee, what are you doing..."

Lee kissed me on the lips and I kissed him back.

The kiss was deep and rough. I tried to break the kiss off, but Lee refused to let me because he became rougher.

The kiss became too rough to the point that I wanted him to stop, but at the same time, I didn't.

I wanted him more than anything in the world right now and I truly did love him. Lee broke the kiss and looked deep into my eyes then at my lips.

"Do you want me to stop?" he asked and I shook my head no, leaving him to continue much rougher than before. His hand was on my waist as we kissed and I could feel my face burning up.

He wouldn't let me catch a breather, not even once. I could tell he was smirking throughout the kiss.

"Lee," I quietly called his name when I got a chance to break the kiss.

"I'll stop."

"What?"

"You can't handle anymore, right?"

"I didn't say anything." "Darling, your face is red."

Lee smirked and grabbed my hand. We started walking and I couldn't believe what had just happened.

Did Lee and I just make out?!

CHAPTER 31

There were many things going through my mind and in my eyes, there were tears. Why did my whole life have to be so confusing and seem so out of place?

I had so many questions, for example, Lee had finally been revealed to me and was the guy I have been seeing in my visions.

I don't understand something. In one of the visions when was I crying, is it because he was leaving?

He gave me a goodbye kiss, but now I see this vision. Was everything out of order?

What was the correct order? I needed to understand everything. Not only that, what plans did my father have? What did Nova know that I didn't?

Why did my mother have to die? Was Blossom going to die next? Who else knew about my past, and who was the mastermind behind everything?

I was freaking out and couldn't take it anymore. I soon realized that the memory of water started to shake.

Shane grabbed my hand and without noticing, we were running together.

"What's happening?"

"The memory of water has woken up. We need to go quickly now."

"You never said anything about this place waking up."

"I did before or did you forget already? I'm guessing you did something to wake it up."

Did I do something? I didn't understand what he meant at all about waking it up.

Was it the memory I saw when I looked deep into the water? Maybe it was too strong and powerful for the water to take.

I let go of Shane's hand and he turned to face me. "What are you doing?"

"You should hurry, since you have limited time. I'm going to stay here."

"No, come with me now."

"I'll find a way to get back."

"Promise?"

I don't know why, but hearing Shane say that he needed to repeat what he just said.

"What did you just say, Shane?"

"DO YOU PROMISE?" He yelled, looking worried as if I wouldn't make it out alive or something.

CHAPTER 32

I looked at him and he said, "Why are you looking at me like that, Chrysan?!"

At first there was no answer from me, but something about his words just seemed familiar.

"CHRYSAN, WHY ARE YOU LOOKING AT ME LIKE THAT?! TELL ME NOW!"

"STOP YELLING AT ME, SHANE!"

"I'LL STOP YELLING IF YOU TELL ME RIGHT NOW!"

"I--"

"DID I DO SOMETHING WRONG, CHRYSAN?! TELL ME?!"

He yelled louder each time and came closer to me, but I kept backing away from him. I knew we should have left, because the island that had memory of water was crumbling.

I couldn't go with Shane, something was very off and I felt like what I was thinking might be right, but what if what I believed was wrong?

"WELL?!"

"Can I ask you something?"

I lowered down my tone, looking scared of him. "ASK AND MAKE IT QUICK!"

"Who--"

"HURRY UP! I HAVE LIMITED TIME HERE AND I CAN'T STAND AROUND DEALING WITH YOU!"

I couldn't believe my ears. Why did he have to be so rude? He's the one who took me here, I never asked to be here in the first place. I laughed right in front of him and he looked really upset.

At the same time the island stopped shaking, but when I turned around, everything was dead.

When I faced Shane, he looked like he was ready to murder someone exactly like how Lee looked.

"Who are you?"

CHAPTER 33

The question, who are you, was a question Lee didn't like being asked.

"Excuse me?"

"You heard me. Who are you?" "Shane," he said.

He looked like he was finally calming down and didn't want to murder someone anymore. I wonder if it was possible that he could be? NO! I should maybe discuss this later with Blossom.

"I don't think you're Shane."

"Why would you say that, Chrysan?"

"You asked if I promised."

"So?"

"Lee said the exact words before."

Flashback

Lee and I were on a date, but he looked sad. "Lee?"

"Yes?" he said in a very sad tone. "What's wrong?"

"Don't worry about it, okay?"

"Are you worried about our relationship again?"

"Yes."

"No matter what happens Lee, I want our relationship to work."

"Promise?"

Lee looked at me and held his pinky finger against mine's

. "Do you promise?"

"Yes. I pinky promise."

Present

"What are you getting at?" "I don't know but…"

"What? You don't know anything, so just mind your business, understand?"

Shane jumped into the water and swam away leaving me on the island, but I knew what I was thinking had to be right!

Am I wrong?

CHAPTER 34

Now let's see how I'll get off this island. I took a deep breath and looked towards the water.

"I guess I'm swimming back," I sighed.

It took me a couple of hours to finally get back and instead of going home, I went straight to Blossom's house. When I arrived, she was outside just watching the night sky. Once she saw me, she started crying.

She ran towards me and hugging me, regardless of how soaked I was.

"Where have you been, Chrysan? I have been so worried about you."

"I'm sorry! Shane took me to a place called, The Memory of Water."

"Did you say Shane?"

I looked at Blossom curiously and asked, "Do you know him?"

Asking that question, she stopped hugging me and backed away slowly. She was mysterious.

"I don't know him."

"Tell me something, Blossom?"

"Tell you what?" she said, clearing her throat. "Do you know who Lee is?"

Blossom looked at me seriously, but at the same time she seemed to know who I was talking about.

"How do you know that name?" she asked.

"The same way you know Shane," I bluntly said, avoiding her question.

"CHRYSAN!"

"Sirius said, I didn't belong to him and he had lost that battle a long time ago. Then, Shane took me to the Memory of Water. I saw a memory of me and Lee. We seemed like we were--"

"In love?"

CHAPTER 35

Blossom and I stared at each other, as I replied yes to her question.

"I do know who Lee is and so do you." "Who is he?"

"Lee is someone you fall in love with. In the past it was forbidden for you two to be together, but you both made it work. He was the love of your life, your everything and finally your boyfriend!

"Seeing the visions and the memories between us, I was even more shocked I couldn't remember a man I loved! My everything!"

"Yes."

"If that's the case, where is he? Did we break up? What happened to him? why can't I remember him?"

"I DON'T KNOW WHERE HE IS!"

I took a step back, as she yelled at me.

"I'm sorry, I didn't mean to yell but I really don't know. You guys didn't break up and I have no idea what happened to him. I can't tell you why you can't remember him."

"Why not?"

"He wouldn't want me to."

"Well, if that's the case, at least tell me what he was like."

She started laughing and I didn't know why, but for a while she wasn't saying anything.

I waited for her to talk again, b u t rain and thunder appeared out of the blue.

Blossom looked scary, I couldn't see her eyes, because she was looking down, smirking.

"You want to know what he was like?" she said coldly.

"Yes."

"He was a—"

"A what?"

"He was a monster and you already knew this, didn't you? Hearing it from someone is different from seeing the monster in him, but you didn't see the true monster inside him."

CHAPTER 36

I was afraid of how she said that and how the thunder struck at the perfect timing. "You're lying."

"Are you ashamed of loving a monster now?" "I--"

Blossom came closer to me and whispered in my ear. "It's funny, because how could a monster ever love you? Maybe he doesn't, which is why he left you that day," *she said coldly.*

My eyes widened from hearing the coldness in Blossom's voice, because how could she ever say that to me?

She was my best friend, so what changed?

I wanted to cry badly, but I decided I wouldn't. I was strong and wouldn't cry for someone who was so cold towards me.

Maybe she was saying this, because of my father?

"Why are you acting like this?"

"Because I can, it's not like we're friends."

"What are you talking about Blossom, we're friends."

"I was never your friend."

"Then, why have you always been so nice to me and pretended you cared about me so much?"

"That was all pretend."

"P-r-e-t-e-n-d?"

"Now that you are learning so much about your past, it's not necessary for me to be your friend anymore." She was lying to me the whole time, why?

Would I be wrong to say she should have died instead of Nova? Nova she was a real friend! Or was she fake like Blossom?

"Ok."

"Glad we agree. We'll say goodbye forever, Chrysan. I won't be seeing you anymore after today."

I took a walk for a while to clear my head before going home.

"Why are you coming back home so late, Chrysan?" my father said, as I walked into the house.

I went over to the fridge and grabbed a bottle of water. My father looked at me as I stood there.

"I'm not going to say, I'm sorry for coming back late."

"Excuse me?"

My father stood up from his chair and he started to look pissed off.

"Are you going to hurt me, just because I didn't apologize?" I laughed.

He laughed, because he could sense I was acting different.

"What is it you want from me?

"I want to be part of your plan now."

"Why the change of heart?"

"Blossom, I thought she was my friend, but she lied to me the whole time."

"What about when I told you that I was threatening her? Did you think she was doing that, because I threatened her?"

"No, because even if she was threatened, she would never listen to a word you say."

I wasn't going to cry like a big baby anymore, because I had enough of everyone, including the person I was talking to.

I was going to figure out everything, whether I needed to use people or not.

A new side of me had awakened and it was not friendly.

CHAPTER 37

I was still involved in my father's plan two months later, but he was being used.

If I'm being honest, I haven't gotten anywhere. He had just been using me for his dirty work and I didn't like it. However, today maybe I could get somewhere.

He told me to pick up wood, but I decided to leave.

I saw the one person I didn't want to see, BLOSSOM!

"Chrysan, what happened to you? You seem so different, even your energy seems off."

I walked away from her, but she grabbed my wrist. There was only silence between us two until I finally turned to look at her with disappointment in my eyes.

"Why are you acting so friendly? We're not friends anymore, remember?"

She grabbed her hair and pulled it off. At first, I wanted to look away from the discussion, but instead shock took over my face.

"There's no way."

I smiled with happiness and I couldn't help, but jump for joy.

I couldn't believe this.

CHAPTER 38

I yelled her name "NOVA!" and then ran into her arms. She was alive and this was so hard to believe, but how was this possible?

"I'm glad I could finally see you again and show you who I was to begin with."

Holding Nova's hands and looking at her, I realized something I said, "You were Blossom all along? WHY?" "I was and I'm sorry. I didn't want to be mean to you, but I needed to pretend to be her or else everyone working for your father would have known that I was not actually dead."

"I don't understand, was Blossom my friend? The clues that were left, was it you? Wait, what you told me before we stopped seeing each other, was that a lie?"

"Let's sit down and talk"

Nova and I sat down where she told me everything.

Nova and Blossom switched places the moment they both were threatened. Neither of them knew death was waiting for one of them.

Then Nova had to pretend to be Blossom, regardless of her being the worst friend, or should I say fake friend to me. The only reason she switched places with Nova in the first place was by force because she thought she wouldn't die first.

"Wait, what about the clues?"

"Clues? I'm sorry, that wasn't me, Chrysan."

"Are you sure? You left some messages and items for me!"

"I'm sure that wasn't me and how would I be able to do most of it? I was with you most of the time. We were looking for clues together."

"I wonder who it could have been?"

Nova and I kept thinking about who it could have possibly been. We couldn't figure it out, but we thought it was a ghost, I laughed and so did she.

Nova said something that made me really think hard. "What if it was your mother?"

I stared into the night sky and my tone became low. "My mother."

"It was a joke!"

"It's fine, but I always had this feeling like she was never dead in the first place."

Nova's eyes widened and I just gazed down.

CHAPTER 39

Nova said, "Do you really believe she's alive?"

"I mean, has anyone gone to her funeral and seen her body?"

"Well, no but—"

"That means she is not dead, she's still alive and my father just lied to me the whole time."

"We wouldn't even know where to start, so do you have any plans?"

"Just keep on pretending to be Blossom and I'll deal with my father's plan. Maybe his plan can help me find my mother."

Nova nodded and we both started walking away, but before she left, I yelled, "THANK YOU FOR POINTING OUT THAT I WASN'T ACTING LIKE MYSELF!"

She waved to me and we went our separate ways. I arrived home and dropped the wood in the back of the house.

"You found a lot of wood, we're going to need it." He told me to go into the house and relax for the rest of the night, so that's what I did.

Who knew what he needed the wood for, but I knew it involved his plan.

After a quick shower, I fell asleep on my bed. Yes, I know you're wondering if I had been in the No Eyes World, since I was the one chosen for some reason.

To answer that question, yes and no. I was not allowed to face Sirius or anyone for that matter, especially if I had changed.

Tonight was different because I didn't go to their world. Instead, there was a fire.

Waking up slowly, I opened my eyes to flames around me, scared for my life that it might end here.

Who? Why? How?

These were the questions I had in mind, like what did I do to deserve this. The fire was everywhere, where could I escape?

*If I touched the fire, I would burn into ashes and it would be the end of me. Suddenly, my eyes became blurry and I started to lose consciousness, passed out into the darkness and into the flames of fire with nowhere to go, no one to call, so **who will be my savior?***

CHAPTER 40

A voice called my name repeatedly.

My eyes wouldn't open, only my ears were listening, but soon enough they gave up on me too. Someone, please save me from this big nightmare.

I didn't want to end my life right now and if I ever did die, let it save the world. A beautiful voice that sounded familiar to me called my name, asking if I could hear after hours and hours of being passed out. Slowly opening my eyes, there was light that was as bright as the sun, but also a woman whom I could barely see.

That was until my eyes were no longer blurry, but fully clear.

To my surprise, the woman wasn't just any random woman, but the person whom I thought was long dead

based on the lies my father had told me. She was standing in front of me.

She wasn't dead, but alive.

The woman was my own mother, the mother who used to tell me bedtime stories about the No Eyes before she was forced to stop by my terrible father.

He wasn't even a real father to me, because he abused me and hurt me in so many ways you couldn't dream of.

How was my own mother alive right now?

"Mother, you're alive! How?"

I cried into her loving arms, wondering how she could have survived.

"I was never dead in the first place and that man thought he killed me, but failed. He was dumb enough not to check if I was still breathing," she said, hugging me tightly.

"That man?"

"I'm talking about your father, darling.

He is not your real father, he never was and I should have told you that from the beginning."

I broke my mother's hug and looked around the room we were in, which was a bedroom, before speaking.

"Mother, do you know who Lee is?"

"I do."

"Can you tell me everything you know? How this man isn't my father because he had abused me so much and it was painful. Then Lee kept appearing in my visions, but I can't remember who he is. Then

there are these other guys, I just don't understand anything anymore."

"I'll tell you everything, but first come with me, we can go somewhere more comfortable to talk."

My mother and I walked out of the bedroom, walking down the hallway where I ran into someone.

I almost fell backwards, but he caught my waist. "Are you okay?" he asked. He was handsome. I nodded my head yes.

He helped me regain my balance again.

"Thank you, I'm okay."

I smiled at him and he walked away. My mother looked at me, grinning.

"Who was that?"

"That's my assistant."

"Assistant? Does he help you around with this huge place?"

"This is a castle and it's ours. He doesn't really help me around, but he does his best, he is blind."

"How is the castle ours and blind, you say? He has a good sense of direction in the castle."

"This is a kingdom for those who are different and you are the princess of this place. It took him years to learn his way around the kingdom and the castle."

"I see, but I'm not different," I said as my mother showed me the kingdom from the balcony.

Everyone looked different and some looked normal, but could be completely different on the inside. I wondered what made me different.

"This is part of the real you, darling, don't be afraid of what you see in this mirror. Now please hold this, but don't look until I tell you to.

My mother came closer to me and removed something from my right eye. I thought maybe it was a piece of hair, but it wasn't.

"Now look."

I looked in the mirror and one of my buttons was missing, but how could that be? Buttons don't come off, especially when you're born with them.

My right eye had no eye.

"You are a button eye and a no eye. You always were since birth, but I had to hide the truth from that man who wasn't your father. Your father is a no eye, and we were in love, but your fake father, Grayson, was in love with me, too. I didn't love him, but he threatened me and your real father. Your father doesn't know why I broke up with him and ended things with him."

I was shocked with what I was hearing. "He threatened to kill him, didn't he? Does my real father know he had a kid?"

"Yes, darling and no, he doesn't know. Nor does your fake father know I'm still alive. He doesn't know if you're

alive either. He thinks he killed you from the fire and he won't check to see."

I knew the whole time that he was never my father and I knew that my mother wasn't dead. I always had a feeling. I was right about Sirius, Shane and Lee too.

"What about Sirius, Shane and Lee, are they--"

"The same person? Yes, they are."

I was right about almost everything, but who is my father? Why was I still the chosen one?

CHAPTER 41

Were they the same person? How? I asked my mother, I wanted to know how this was possible.

"If you really must know…"

My mother told me that his real name was Lee.

Lee's parents, when we were younger, Lee's parents did an experiment on him. An experiment that would split him into two other versions of himself.

Each version would represent a part of Lee.

Doing this experiment was the biggest mistake of their life, because three versions of him turned on the parents.

How?

The experiment messed up Lee's way of thinking, making the third version of him a monster. They truly had created one by making different versions of him.

He thought he had control.

She told me that I never noticed that they were the same until now. All of them were pretty good at hiding it.

I had already met all three of them in the past, just like my visions showed.

The version of Lee I fell in love with was the monster I kissed goodbye.

"Does he still love me?" I asked, but my mother replied as if she didn't know.

No one knew where Lee was, but the other two versions of him had been found.

"One thing, darling, you must know— Lee's parents worked with Grayson."

My jaw dropped! Did that mean Lee was working with my fake father, or had he worked with him when we were together? I wonder, did that mean the reason he never wanted to hear about the No Eyes was because one of Lee's versions was one? Since the three versions of Lee turned on him, including the No Eyes, it could be the reason he dislikes them.

Everything was starting to be clear and I understood things better. I needed to show my father, my real father, who I was.

I needed to show No Eyes as well, even if it meant revealing myself to Sirius.

In my eyes, he wasn't Lee, only SIRIUS! "You should go to them now."

"All I have to do is go to sleep again and I'll be there?"

"Yes, don't worry, you'll return here safely."

CHAPTER 42

The moment I fell asleep, the castle of the queen and king of the No Eyes was right in front of me.

Before entering, I covered my right eye so no one would see it. I walked into the castle without permission.

They were having a meeting.

The guards tried to stop me, but I was able to get past them. "Why are you here again, Chrysan?" Sirius said, looking furious.

"I am not here for you, but I am here to find my real father."

Everyone looked at me like I was weird.

"Dear, what are you talking about? You are a button eye. You have a father, and he abuses you. I believe you are confused," Queen Widow spoke.

"I am not."

I removed my right hand from my right eye, showing everyone in the room that I was one of them.

They were all shocked and I didn't blame them because they never saw anything like it.

I was the only button-eye-no-eye anyone had ever seen. "How is this possible?" Sirius asked, and I explained everything to them.

It was weird, because there was a guard who kept looking at me and I didn't realize until looking back at him that he kind of looked like me.

He was the same guard, who was in the hospital room with me.

I went up to the guard and asked if he knew my mother. "You're my daughter?" he asked and suddenly, he hugged me tightly.

Listen! I don't hug or talk to strangers, but this feeling was a bond of a father and a daughter finding each other.

After being hidden for such a long time, I hugged my father back and cried.

My green and black tears came out, but I didn't care. No Eyes had to accept me for being different.

All that mattered to me was that I had found my real father.

"I'm so happy that I found you, because I came here for what I needed to do. You should come with me to see my mother."

"I can't leave so quickly, this is my home Chrysan, regardless if you are my daughter or not."

"It's okay, you should go be with your family and take all this in," King Shadow said, taking a deep breath.

Before leaving, I turned to Sirius and smiled at him. "Looks like you were right. I was one of you guys the whole time. No wonder you felt like I was."

"Yea—"

CHAPTER 43

Back to the kingdom. My father and I entered the castle. Walking in, he looked amazed to see this kingdom that was created just for those who were different.

I was surely happy about that, since I was one of those people who were different.

"This castle is where you live?" he asked. "Yes."

I nodded my head. "You are back?"

My father looked up and saw my mother standing on the stairwell. He was truly happy to see her. I could tell he missed her, regardless of them being forced to end their relationship.

"I brought father back, hoping you two could talk.

I'll just be in our library, if you need me" I said walking away.

A couple of hours passed reading in the library and I didn't realize it was getting late. "Hey" a familiar voice spoke and I turned to see my mother's assistant. "Hello!

I'm sorry I never got your name. What is it?"

"My name is Shay and your name is Chrysan, correct?"
"Yes, did my mother tell you my name?"

"Yeah, she told me a lot about you over the years."

"I see do you want to sit down or are you going to stand the whole time?"

"I'll sit."

I watched him as he touched the items that were beside him and in front. He was struggling, but soon enough he was able to find the chair next to me.

"How did you become blind?" I accidentally said, randomly thinking why I asked that.

"I—,"

I tried to stop him from telling me, because it was a mistake to ask, but he kept talking anyway. "I was born blind!"

On the day of my birth there was an accident, causing this to happen to me. I also lost my mother and father as well."

Hearing him talk about how he lost his family was sad. He didn't have anyone but my mother, but now he has me. Just because he was some blind kid didn't mean anything.

He was still a person with No Eye. He should be welcomed with open arms, regardless of him being different.

"I'm sorry to hear what happened, but you're not alone. You have me and my mother. If that's not enough, I'm sure we can find people who will accept you for who you are." Shay thanked me for being so kind and loving towards him. We talked to each other for the rest of the night. I learned so much about him and I started to feel safe with him.

What did it mean? Did I fall in love with him? I just met him, so that's not possible unless I only like him as a CRUSH!

He walked me to my bedroom and said goodnight. Before he walked away, I stopped him.

"What's wrong?"

"Nothing, it's just I wanted to ask a question."

"You haven't finished asking questions? Okay, go ahead."

"What's your type of girl?"

"Do you mean my ideal type?"

"Yes."

Shay smirked and walked closer to me, pinning me to the wall. Even though he was blind, he still knew what he was doing.

"Shay? What are you doing?" I asked, flustered by his actions.

"I can't believe you asked what my ideal type was. Instead of me telling you, how about I show you instead?" "How?" I questioned and he pressed his lips against mine. He was kissing me and the kiss felt magical.

Shay didn't even let me take a breather not even once, until he was done kissing me.

"I'll have to steal some more kisses from you tomorrow, goodnight."

"Goodnight," I said, melting on the floor, amazed at what had just happened.

Did this mean he was going to do this every day? Kiss me out of nowhere or was he teasing me for fun?

He was driving me crazy and I couldn't take it! The way he kissed was something else, something I had never felt before.

CHAPTER 44

The next day, I woke up to my mother in my closet. I asked her what she was doing in my room, she said she was picking an outfit out for me.

I didn't understand why, but the way she was smiling meant, "I'M GOING ON A DATE!" I yelled and she nodded.

The only person who could have planned this was Shay.

I mean, we kissed yesterday. I finished up and went downstairs. There he was, Shay. He looked nice.

"You look really beautiful." he said, slowly grabbing my hand.

"Thank you, you look nice too. It's too bad you can't see it with your own eyes.

Shay ignored me and just told me we should get going.

I was pretty sure that it bothered him, but I didn't say anything. Feeling the pain in my chest, I thought that it was a pity that he couldn't see what I saw. This kingdom was my kingdom, it was perfect. "Can I ask you a question, Shay?"

"Go ahead."

"What would…?"

I wasn't able to talk for some reason and luckily it was just us, so no one would see the tears coming out of my eye.

It had to relate to the question that I wanted to ask.

"You don't have to cry tears of black or green. Be brave and breathe. Although it may be hard to see, I believe in you. I am proud of you for being able to figure it all out on your own. Even when you were at your toughest and lowest, you still did it," he said when tear after tear came out my eyes.

My chest was in pain, my heart was broken. He was good a speaking true words.

He hugged me tightly and didn't want to let go. "You wanted to ask me what I would do if I knew that the end was coming for me?"

"Yes," I whispered, still crying my heart out.

"It depends, could I dye from saving the world, or for no reason at all?"

"Die saving the world?"

"I won't do anything."

"Why?" I said, breaking the hug and staring at him even if he couldn't see me.

"I wouldn't have any regrets, since I was the one who saved the world."

"What if you didn't want to save the world? Would you still think like this? Does your life NOT MATTER AT ALL TO YOU?"

"I will always give you the same answer Chrysan. You ask me this because you know that you are the chosen one. Those who are chosen to save the world are never able to survive."

He was right about everything. I asked, because I didn't want to be chosen, nor did I want to save the world.

The cave I was in had all those who were the chosen ones and they never made it back to see their loved ones.

Instead, they are in heaven or in the sky, FOREVER GONE! That's why they all said goodbye.

I have to admit, I was afraid to die. Why? I wouldn't be able to stand the screaming or crying of those who loved me, because they would witness my skin peeling and my body going cold.

I wouldn't be able to stand those who knew the truth about everything and pretend like they truly cared about me, when they worked for the man I called my father.

I wouldn't be able to leave the one that I began to fall in love with, even if we met for a short amount of time.

I do know this, I'm going to be able to say those three words, ***"I love you,"*** *before I ever die!*

CHAPTER 45

Our lips pressed against each other for just a few seconds. I didn't notice his lips on mine.

After all of this, we continued the date and we had the best time ever, more fun then when we kissed.

Today was supposed to be the day where I found courage to be brave and take being chosen one to heart. I was able to have this and no one else did, but ME!

I shouldn't be ashamed of being chosen and it was crazy how Shay had to show that to me.

It made me think, if he could have been the one to save the world too? A blind No Eye saves the world.

We walked through the kingdom, all eyes were on us. You could hear the whispers how Shay was the blind boy who couldn't see.

It made him different from the rest, maybe because he was the only one?

Around the end of the date, we returned to the castle and my parents were happy with each other despite being apart for so long. They asked us how the date was, but we both shook our heads, saying it was good.

I wasn't sure what was wrong with Shay, because he walked away from me so quickly. I hoped he was okay.
"Chrysan, can you come here?" *Mother asked.*

Father walked in the same direction as Shay.

My mother and I stayed here.

"Is everything okay?"

"Did something happen between you and Shay?"

"It's not that important, but does he not like me?"

"You're funny, of course he likes you. He may not show it well, but he does, so don't take his coldness to heart."

"What about Lee?"

"Lee does not deserve you. You need to forget about him for good and focus on someone who truly has feelings for you. Shay is lucky to have you and you are lucky to have him.

I can tell you he will love you with every single beat of his heart.

He will be that type of boyfriend or husband who will wonder what you're doing, where you are and if you are safe. He may be blind, but he'll do anything to protect the one he loves, which is you."

"If you can talk about Shay like that, then it's not wrong for me to catch feelings for him, even if he'll be judged by others. It shouldn't matter because love is love, right?"

"That's right and you should always remember that."

"THANK YOU!" I said and hugged her.

I went upstairs to find Shay and when I did, he was in front of my room door. He looked up at me.

"Shay."

"I don't want you to talk or anything, okay? Just listen!"

"Okay."

"I'm starting to catch feelings for you, Chrysan. I know I'm blind and I do struggle to find my way, but you still like me for me. You are caring and kind, you don't judge. I can't see you, but I bet you're beautiful."

"I thought I was the only one who started to feel those feelings. You are different from all the other guys I have met.

Your personality is truly something special and I love it."

"I'm glad you do, now come here." I went over to him and we hugged.

Shay whispered in my ear and asked me to be his girlfriend.

We might be moving fast and we rushed this relationship, but we are not going to say we love each other, only that we are simply like each other.

Let's see what the future has in store for the both of us.

CHAPTER 46

A couple of months later we were all still living a happy life. My parents were happy, too.

I was still with Shay, while those two remarried one another. We had fun together for the past months, so I didn't remember I had something to do as the chosen one. Someone appeared at our castle one day. Wondering who it was? There was only one person I left and had forgotten, since the house caught fire.

That person was my best friend, NOVA!

"Thank goodness, I found you. I was so worried about you," she said, running up to me, hugging me tightly.

I looked over at my mother and she looked a little scared. I was not sure why, but if she was scared, I should be too.

"How did you find this place?" my mother said, coldly.

Nova backed away from me, because she was afraid of my mother.

"I was just looking everywhere for this place and came across some vines. I went through them and ended up here. Why?"

"Did you watch your surroundings?"

"What do you mean by my surroundings?"

"There are many ways you can arrive in my kingdom, but that way is the easiest. If anyone followed you or watched you enter and never came back out, they could find this place and come through themselves. We all would be in danger because of you."

"How would we be in danger, Mother?"

"Do you truly believe, that because Grayson wants to kill all the NO EYES that he wouldn't want to hurt more people? If he finds out that me and you are alive, he will turn on our people as well."

"I didn't think about that at all. You just want everyone in this Kingdom to be safe, but it shouldn't be just us."

"Chrysan, are you saying that you are ready to fight now?" Shay asked, holding my hand.

"I am, after all Dad has been teaching me how to fight and use weapons. Not only that, but everyone in the Kingdom has been learning to fight."

"Are you sure you are ready to be the chosen one?" she asked worriedly.

"Yes, and I'm pretty sure Nova here wanted to remind me of just that. I'm assuming things have gotten worse back home?"

"Yes, bad! Everyone is on his side, despite not knowing the real him. Now they are going to use some sort of magic, so they can attack the NO EYES without them knowing."

"When are they planning to attack?"

"Umm, actually they plan to attack in four days, if nothing goes wrong in their plan."

"If that's the case, we will just have to make sure everyone is ready to fight and those who aren't, we must get them to safety."

"We should get prepared right away, meaning right now," Shay mentioned.

Everyone had to be ready and I had to be prepared for what was to come for me during this fight.

Not that I wanted this to happen, but many lives would be lost, but they would be remembered for fighting for their kingdom.

CHAPTER 47

I went to the No Eyes world to warn the queen and king about what was happening with Shay. They were all very concerned about the problem, but knew war was coming eventually. They were already prepared for war. The queen and king gave orders to the guards to get their people to safety, Sirius came up to me.

"Who is this?" he asked.

I could tell that he was jealous of Shay. Why? He probably expected me to be with Lee.

Maybe he didn't know he was another version of him.

"I'm her boyfriend," Shay spoke bluntly and the look on Sirius's face was FURIOUS!

"Chrysan, shouldn't you be dating Lee right now instead of him?"

"Lee is old news Sirius, I'm much happier with Shay. If you're trying to tell me who I should be with, it means you don't know the truth about yourself."

"You shouldn't be my love, some things should be left unspoken."

"What are you talking about?"

"You are" I started to say until a voice cut me off. It wasn't just a random voice, but a familiar voice.

"You are one version of me." he said.

Turning around, I saw all the memories come back again. It was the real Lee, the Lee I had fallen in love with, the Lee I kissed before all of this happened.

"Lee?" I whispered his name quietly and he walked up to me.

Shay wasn't pleased to see Lee standing there in front of me. He didn't want me to fall in love with him all over again, but I wouldn't, at least I don't think so.

"It's good to see you again, Chrysan. I missed you a lot and wanted to see your face again," he said, gently grabbing my hand and kissing it.

I removed my hand and started to feel angry. "How can you just show up now?!"

"What?"

"Lee, you do understand you left me and made me forget about you. You left me no choice, but to forget. Then, I find out that I met all three versions of you leaving me and having you in every corner. FOR WHAT?! To fall in love with one version of you."

"It's not like I wanted to, Chrysan. I never wanted to leave, but there was no choice. I had been looking for you forever."

"You expect me to believe that? You knew exactly where to find the other versions of you, so you could have easily found me. I didn't miss you, not one bit! In fact, Shay here is my boyfriend, not you."

"Why are you being so harsh? I didn't come here to argue with you, okay, I just wanted to help fight with you and everyone else to put a stop to Grayson."

"No, we don't need your help."

"Chrysan, just let him help and worry about this later. We don't have enough time for this, okay?" Shay whispered in my ear and I agreed to let Lee help us just this once. Afterwards, I won't have to see his face anymore. "You're me?" Sirius asked, and Lee nodded his head yes. While all of us continued preparing to fight, those two went off to find Shane. They all wanted to have a talk, since they were one and the same.

"You aren't mad at me, right?" I asked Shay and he replied no, but said, I should've been more mature about the situation.

He wasn't wrong.

Focusing should have been the only thing to worry about, considering we were all about to go to war soon. The world needs saving, not endless arguments over the past. Someone needed to slap me, so I wouldn't cause any problems.

CHAPTER 48

The day of the war was finally here. In just two hours, the fight will begin and everyone was ready. Those who weren't going to help fight were safe and sound. There was no more playing around, because the time had come to put an end to this fake father of mine.

I decided that I would tell him I wasn't his real daughter and never was. I would be super happy with his reaction when he saw the family was back together. "Are you ready to fight?" *Father said, sitting next to me.*

I didn't reply until I was ready to speak. "I was nervous but ready."

"No need to be nervous, everyone has each other's back including those you dislike at the moment."

"What if everything goes wrong? What if we lose this fight against him?"

"We won't, as long as you believe and trust that we can fight together like we are one."

"I don't want to see the people I love die or end up hurt. I'm not sure what I would do if that happened."

"How about you rest? It will take your mind off things."

"Okay, thank you."

I laid down in bed and my father left. I didn't sleep for that long, just about 20 minutes or so.

When I got out of my bed, I decided to write a letter to everyone and sneak it in their pocket or somewhere else.

"Shouldn't you be resting right now, my love?"

I hid everything quickly before turning around. It was Shay standing there.

I was startled but it wasn't necessary for me to hide them since it was only Shay.

He was blind after all and wasn't able to see what I was doing.

"How did you know I was awake?"

"I could hear you writing."

"Oh, sorry!"

"What were you writing?"

"Just writing about how much I love you." I lied to him and that was wrong of me.

"Cute."

"So why did you come?"

"I wanted to hear your voice before the fight began or maybe even a little more."

I stood up from my chair and walked towards him. We hugged one another.

"I am happy you came, I was starting to wonder when you would show up."

"Why is that?" he smirked.

"I started to miss you."

"You have no idea how much you make me fall in love with you again and again."

"I just want you to kiss me, like there's no turning back."
"Is that what you wish for me to do?"

"Yes," I whisper, coming closer to his lips, brushing against them.

"If that's what you truly want, my love, I'll kiss you a million times until you tell me to stop."

"Don't stop."

He closed the gap between our lips. The feeling of his lips kissing mine never got old. I was deeply in love with him that it was sad, because this would be our last kiss.

We both broke the kiss and I said, "I love you."

Saying those three words was the most important thing that someone could say, because you never know what might happen next.

"I love you too and I will never stop."

In the next hour, it would be time for war and somebody was going to die, but who?

Or more so, how many?

CHAPTER 49

Everyone was in their fighting position, because the war was about to begin. I could tell everyone was either afraid or ready to put an end to this.

I looked over at Shay and he looked ready. "Shay, are you sure you want to do this?" I whispered.

"I'm sure, I will not back down when this war is about to begin. There is no running away from what has only just begun."

"Right."

"Everyone 10… 9…. 8… 7… 6… 5… 4… 3…. 2… and 1."

We were right on time, because Grayson and the others rushed into action, but they weren't the only ones.

The fight was dead even, though it had just started.

People were already dying and it was painful to see.

As we fought, Grayson quietly slipped away somewhere and I followed him. "Chrysan? Where are you?" Shay asked.

"I'm still here, but I have to follow Grayson and see what he is up to."

"Go."

"What no, I can't just leave you. Come with me."

"I'll be okay."

"But——."

"Don't worry, me and the other guys have his back" Lee spoke and I rolled my eyes.

"Why would I trust him? You know what fine, but if anything happens to him, you're DEAD!"

I started to leave, but I felt someone grab my hand. "Before you go, always remember that I love you and I'll never stop. Just focus on ending this and try not to worry about everyone here," Shay said.

He almost gave me one more kiss, but we were interrupted because of the blood being spattered.

I left to follow Grayson, but when I entered the castle, I lost sight of him. Suddenly, someone kicked me from behind and I fell on the ground.

It was Grayson.

He picked my bow and arrow up, keeping it with him. He pointed his sword at me and laughed. "I see you are still alive, but you're missing a button eye, my dear daughter." "I'm not your daughter." I said, getting back on my feet.

"You are."

"I am not! Mother, she sewed that fake button into my eye to make you think I was your real daughter. Not only that, but my real father knows me and now they both are together again."

"Your mother is alive? How?"

"You should always check if someone is alive or dead, but you didn't, so that's why."

He started laughing and called out as if he was calling out to someone.

There were others pointing weapons at me, coming closer. I should have brought backup with me.

"You truly believe that you know everything? Everyone out there will die and it will be because of you."

"That's not true."

"How would you know? You are not out there with them, but instead you chose to follow me."

What he was saying was right. I could have been helping my family, friends and my lover, but I followed him, leaving them all alone. What was wrong with me? I did not even

notice that everyone had disappeared around me and someone came from behind me, hitting me on the head with something hard.

Being so blind, I was knocked out cold on the ground.

CHAPTER 50

I started to wake up after a few minutes, but heard a voice. It didn't sound like anyone who knew me, but it was a male. He looked like he was 18 and he was a Button Eye.

I never saw him around before and didn't think he was one of the people who wanted to help. "Who are you?"

"Oh, I'm sorry! I didn't mean to be rude. My name is Timmy and you're Chrysan, right?"

"Yes, but how do you know my name?"

"Well, I heard about you from the other button eyes, but don't worry, I mean the good ones."

"She's awake."

Nova ran and hugged me tightly. Mother, father, Shay and a few others were there too. "Where is everyone else?" I asked and everyone became quiet.

"My love, they all are dead."

My eyes widened from hearing those words. How could they be dead?

"What?"

"That includes Lee, Sirius and Shane too."

"Everyone died protecting either someone they loved about or you."

"Are you saying Lee died protecting Shay?"

"That's correct, my love. He kept his word about making sure nothing was to happen to me."

My heart broke and I started crying. Why did I cry? I'm not sure. I wasn't in love with Lee anymore, but only Shay. Or was it the thought that I was knocked out and everyone was still fighting?

After I finished crying, they told me Timmy found me and them as well. The fight wasn't over yet until we stopped my fake father, but no one knew where he was.

"We can still do this," I said, putting a brave face on.

Even though we lost so many people, Timmy was now willing to help us.

CHAPTER 51

When we found Grayson and the others, we first figured out what he was planning. He was trying to find out the other locations to the other worlds, so he could kill every single person there who didn't want to obey him as the new king. The main location he wanted to appear in was a kingdom called the Dream Kingdom.

There were different species and creatures that wasn't anything like us.

As soon as a few of them were gone, we all split up, but my mother and father decided they would take Grayson on instead of me.

They wanted to pay him back for hurting me. I needed to fight twice as hard, because everyone had cuts and bruises all over them unlike me, who barely had a scratch. Timmy and I were paired up to fight together, regardless whether we knew each other.

He saved my life. Everyone kept fighting and fighting. Meanwhile, we had to figure out what to do to stop Grayson.

Something was weird, because everyone came back rushing at me, including Shay. I was confused, but my mother said "Step away from him."

"Why, Mother?"

"He is not our friend, he is our enemy."

"I'm not sure I understand."

"Grayson is dead, but before he died he said you were in danger and asked if you met a boy named Timmy.

He is an enemy."

I looked towards Timmy.

He wasn't saying a word, but smiling instead.

"Timmy?"

"I don't know what they're talking about, Chrysan. These people are crazy. I saved you, remember? So why I would want to hurt you?"

Everything felt off and I was confused, even trying to walk over to Shay.

I felt something sharp came through my body. Blood was coming out of my mouth and my vision

flashed before my eyes. Everyone screamed and ran to me while Timmy smirked, he watched me fall to the ground.

I didn't realize until now that Grayson wasn't the one behind any of this to begin.

It was no other than his son, the MASTERMIND behind all of this.

CHAPTER 52

I know it's crazy to believe. Grayson had a son? It doesn't make any sense, right?

When he left the house that day, he looked like he was talking to someone, but I didn't know who it was.

I bumped into someone, but no one was there. I felt like I was being watched. The person I heard was talking to Nova's parents about her death and so for many more reason why Timmy was the mastermind.

He was perfect for the job, because he looked like this sweet innocent person, but truly he wasn't. No one would have ever suspected him, not even me.

In this story he played the hero, but on the outside he was the worst villain.

"Why didn't I realize this sooner?" I quietly said.

Everyone was panicking, but Shay calmed them down. Some of them went to find first aid to see if that could help, while the others stayed with me.

"What did you not realize?" Father asked. "Timmy, he was always there watching me." "There?"

"Yes, the whole time."

"What?"

"He saw everything."

I gave a gentle smile and slowly closed my eyes, but they kept me awake.

They wanted me to make it, but who was to say I could? Every single one of them thought back into their memory, trying to see if they had watched or experienced the same as me, realizing that he was there.

When they fell on their knees, the letters I wrote fell with them. I saw them pick them up and started reading, knowing that it was written by me. This was my way of saying goodbye. One by one, they read their letter and each of them cried.

The only one who didn't cry was Shay.

"Shay, you have one too…." Nova said while picking the letter up.

"Can you read it?" he asked and Nova stood there looking at him before saying anything.

"Are you sure?"

"I want to hear it before I lose the love of my life."

"WE WON'T LOSE HER!" She yelled, but the truth was no one was able to help.

The blood was too heavy and I was losing too much. "I'll read it."

CHAPTER 53

My father took the letter from Nova's hand, taking a deep breath before reading it out loud.

My Love Shay,

I haven't known you for that long, just a couple of months, to tell you the truth that's okay. I have fallen deeply in love with you and I'm happy to call you mine. By the time that you read this I will already be fading away. I'll be gone, so read this and remember me.

You showed me why I should wonder what being chosen and being different would be like. Many are never chosen and wasn't ever going to be one, even if they were just like you.

You should have been chosen, not me. I didn't believe I had a courage to save the world. Anyway, this isn't about being chosen. I will find you again, no matter how long it takes. No matter how many lifetimes, I will find all of you. I'll know it's you, because we are soulmates, at least that's what I think and hope to believe.

I'll wait for you and love you forever up until my last breath. I adore you and I love you. Please stay

strong for me and I didn't write this to hurt you, but I saw death in my own eyes. I don't want to say goodbye, but this is just the beginning for now.

Let my tears of black and green drop every single time you all cry, including you.

Love,

Chrysan

Shay never cried until now. He might be blind, but he sure could cry just as much as me and the others. I would never forget any of them and I would always come back as the chosen one.

No one would stop until everything was put to an end. That means those who carried evil would be gone for good. Even if I was not there, a new chosen one would be born and they would go through a huge mystery, just like me.

"Don't you dare say goodbye, Chrysan, I love you too much for this!"

No one wanted me to say goodbye, so I didn't.

With my last view of everyone, I took my last hug, last kiss and last breath.

I'm not saying goodbye, but I'm saying,

"Button Eyes, No Eyes."

THE END

ACKNOWLEDGMENT

Hello everyone, my name is Monet Tyson.

I finished this book at age 16 on August 3rd, 2023. This book was started on March 19th, 2023. I hope you will enjoy reading my first book, I had a great support system on my side. I'm grateful for my family and friends, especially my grandmother (Audrey Tyson), who has always sacrificed for our family.

Also, I thank God for letting me use my gifts to share this book to all the readers in the world. God bless everyone and please follow me on social media, so you can stay tuned in on what's coming next!

Where to find the author:

Wattpad: @Monettyson.
Pinterest: @ShiningDreamingly.
YouTube: @ShiningDreamingly.
Zepeto: @ShiningDreamingly.
TikTok: @ShiningDreamingly.

www.ingramcontent.com/pod-product-compliance
Lightning Source LLC
LaVergne TN
LVHW021828060526
838201LV00058B/3554